"Bad girls aren't villains; they're transgressive forces within patriarchal cultures. Made to choose between wreaking destruction and accepting their own powerlessness, they pick destruction."

— *Judy Berman*

You Were Married When I Met You

poems by
rebecca rijsdijk

for the other women

Contents

Foreword

Cold Bones 10

Sharp Skins 11

Rafts built of Firewood 12

Stones 13

If You Love Them 14

City Lights 16

Quick Sand 17

Let it Burn... 18

The Hurt 24

Dragons and dark haired Boys 27

Ball and Chain 28

Fire Starter 30

Woman Up 32

Phoenix 34

Scraps 35

Goodnight You Say.. 36

Paris, or the Last Time I Saw You.. 37

Spine.. 38

Moon	39
Daddy	40
To the Bone	42
Dogs and Masters	44
When Hope is a Lot Like a Loaded Gun	46
Truth	47
'Crazy Woman'	48
The Fantasy of You and Me	50
All was Never Well	51
Carpaccio	52
The Healing	54
Not About You	56
Rejection Abandonment	57

A Lie

About the Author

Recommended Reading

Foreword

This is a small book of poetry about being 'the other woman.' It brings me closure in one of the most difficult situations I ever dealt with in my life.

Contrary to popular belief 'the other woman' isn't some mythical she-monster with snakes for hair. Neither is she a 'slut' or a 'homewrecker.' Sometimes she's just a nursing assistant working 12,5-hour shifts picking up other people's poop. Sometimes she is the one in the shadows, picking emotionally unavailable partners to recreate a childhood dynamic filled with rejection and abandonment.

This booklet is not about him, I forgave him a long time ago. It's about the women who are ashamed of speaking up; who are ashamed of being stigmatised by a patriarchal society. It is for women like me, who try to lick their wounds in all the wrong places.

If this is you; I want you to know you are worthy of love, the real deal, the unconditional love stuff from a man that will be single when you meet him, but above all, the love you will give yourself after you kiss all the bullshit and the hurt goodbye and start walking on the road to recovery.

You, my love, were never alone.

You Were Married When I Met You

Cold Bones

It was one
of those days
where it was spring
in the sunshine
and winter
in the shadows.

I wait for you
at the bus stop
just in case
she is there too
and I can pretend
to be a traveler.

I wait and wait
until I slowly disappear
into the crowd.

I start walking
and only stop
when i reach the spot
where the sun
hits the pavement
and warms
my aching
bones.

Rebecca Rijsdijk

Sharp Skins

sharp skins
it said
on the blue
fabric
of the train
seat

sharp
skins

and i know
of which
the vandal
spoke

skin
so soft
the mere memory
of touching it
cuts you like
a thousand knives
and leaves you
dreaming
about dying

You Were Married When I Met You

Rafts built of Firewood

i wonder
whether
i am
the only one
in love
as i
stand here
on the shoreline
watching you
drift away
on a raft
built from firewood
and broken promises
obsessively clinging on
to the ghosts
from your past

Rebecca Rijsdijk

Stones

you broke my heart
and pissed on it
while spitting
in my face

You Were Married When I Met You

If You Love Them

i held on for so long
because i thought
you were the real deal
and that your words
would align with your actions
one day
that you were just struggling
to become the man
i saw glimpses of
every now and then

and there you were
two months after
the silence
saying things like
'It's just life'

brushing away
any responsibility
to the wife
you cheated on
and the seeds
you planted
in my heart

if you love them

set them free

and when i finally
saw your true colours
the shutters came down
like the castle gates in one
of those medieval movies
and you went from
being 'the one'
to being just another clown
who talks the talk
but will never walk the walk

and i pity you for it

You Were Married When I Met You

City Lights

and now
you are but
a shadow
in a dream
as i cling
to an image

fading

your face
the city lights
reflecting
on the river
when
you kissed me
in public
for the first time

always
in the shadows

Rebecca Rijsdijk

Quick Sand

it took me years
to realise
i had been trying
to build our home
on quicksand
all this time

You Were Married When I Met You

Let it Burn

the world is burning
and i am still
crying
about a boy
with two faces
happy to serve
all those who
pay
tribute
with their
words

the world is burning
and i don't get out
of bed until noon
drinking g&t's
in my pyjamas
on my days off work

i still go to work mum
shining for the elderly
who complain
about things like
someone cheating
at a card game

Rebecca Rijsdijk

and
did
you
see
what
mrs so
and so
was
wearing

the world is burning
and i eat my way
through packets
of citalopram
flushed down
with energy drinks
and cigarettes
cleaning up
the human waste
my patients
leave behind

i am a highly
functioning
depressed
piece of
shit
i tell my therapist

You Were Married When I Met You

she says i have
to be nicer to myself

the world is burning
and an area as big as
several european
countries combined
went up in flames
in australia today
millions of animals
with it
and eighteen people
gone
and the prime minister's
response was
'ban all climate activism
because my privileged
white friends are
getting upset
about destroying the planet'

and why the fuck would he care
he lives in New Zealand anyway

lock them up
all of them
the orange baboon
the rocket man
the bankers

Rebecca Rijsdijk

and eaton boys
lock them up
take their money
and save our
fucking planet

the world is burning
i watch the news
on my telephone
because the television
lies a lot
and so do the papers
because they're all
owned by a greedy
old white man
who hates the world

speaking of white

i get called white privileged
by a stranger on the internet
who calls himself
a decent man
until i finally said 'no'

i project enough
shit on myself
as it is
thank you

You Were Married When I Met You

very
very
much

the world is burning
and i go back to bed
because today
someone else
has to take responsibility
for shouting things like

'hold them accountable
ban fossil fuels
hang the tory scum'

the world is burning
and i watch a boy take a train
apparently it a big deal
because he is the a model
hashtag live se because
she skipped her tyhopper flight
to blog about tag
a train to a city urope
to photograph fion
which also happ to be
one of the biggest luting industries
in the world hash whatever

and he forgot abou

Rebecca Rijsdijk

all the times he took
the train with me
because today was his
first time too
or so he said

the two faced lying cunt

the world is burning
and my tongue
hurts of all the things
i did not say
to his perfect
litte face

i just swallow the ashes

the world is burning

and
so
am
i

You Were Married When I Met You

The Hurt

you know
after all
this time
and all this pain
i still love him
i said

i could see
in her eyes
that she knew
what i was talking
about

than you probably
always will

does it get better

the sharp edges
will come off

but the hurt
will stay
i asked

it will be there

Rebecca Rijsdijk

she replied
but more
like
an undercurrent

my beeper goes
her eyes
come back
to the here
and now
the brightly lit
corridor of a
seventies built
carehome

it's room three o six
i mumble

then you'd better go
before she smears
the contents of her
pad all over the wall again

we part
in opposite directions
and i wonder
who's name
it was
carved

You Were Married When I Met You

in the dark corners
of her heart

where her
undercurrent
was running

and if she
sometimes
called her husband
by the other person's
name

Rebecca Rijsdijk

Dragons and dark-haired Boys

i sleep holes
into the day
dreaming about
dragons
and dark haired
boys
who stay

You Were Married When I Met You

Ball and Chain

we will always
be lovers he said
we will just not
be together

release me
is what he
meant
you drive me nuts
is what he meant
i can't handle
your love
is what he meant

and i just
have to let go
of this imaginary
ball and chain
he made me
keeper of
the ball and chain that
were never grounded
anywhere
but in his twisted
version of reality

and with it
my love

Fire Starter

it was my father
who taught me
that love was not
unconditional
but that it had to be
earned
like everything else
in life

your father taught you
that you were
unlovable
that you needed
to man up
get a steady job
pay the bills
die quietly
no wave making

ripple effect

life

but you
my love
were always

meant to be
a fire starter

and this is why
you would never
stay

You Were Married When I Met You

Woman Up

i woke up angry today

this still happens
sometimes

and it's because of you
and it's because of me
and i am sick
of being the empathetic one
the one who understands
the one who waits
the one who has infinite
amounts of goddamned
wasted patience

you're scared
you say
you don't want a relationship
you say
you tried
you say

and i say something
about your daddy
and your mummy
and i say something

about your wife
And your trauma
and your emotional
unavailafuckingbility

but what i really
want to say
is that we
are all scared

some of us
just woman
the fuck up

You Were Married When I Met You

Phoenix

i dreamed of fire and smoke
standing in a disappearing room
eaten away by flames

the floors started giving away
when i saw you
slumped in a chair
dead as a doornail
apparently having
started it all

the sparks of destruction
still igniting
from your fingertips

i can feel my lungs
slowly fill with the dust
of what once was
as my throat
starts to burn
and it is then
i realise
there's no point
in coughing
for i too
am already dead

Rebecca Rijsdijk

Scraps

i mistook
your scraps
for solid
gold

You Were Married When I Met You

Goodnight
You Say

i think about you
all the time
i say

goodnight you say

i love you
i say

did you read the news
about brexit
you ask

i miss you i say
you send me a video
of a dancing dog
in reply

it hurts
i say

and then
there is nothing
but silence

Rebecca Rijsdijk

Paris, or the Last Time I Saw You

i hate myself, he said
his long black hair
still damp from the shower

we used to shower together
but today i walked out
of the bathroom
when he walked in

i love you, i replied
taking his head in my hands
i love you
i love you
i love you

i kiss him
until the tears stop
and then we say
goodbye

You Were Married When I Met You

Spine

you have to let it go
they say

(but only because they love me)

but i am still angry
and in pain
i feel things
so deeply
i cry about shit
i see on the
television

and then i think
of my sister's words

she spoke them
over the phone

you already have one
spineless man
in your life
she said

why would you need
another one

Rebecca Rijsdijk

Moon

she looked
at the moon

and it was full
and bright
where she was

she looked
at the moon
and thought
of the boy
and how he
had said
it was cloudy
where he was
and how his heart
felt heavy
like a starless
night

but it was
still beating

You Were Married When I Met You

Daddy

my father
gave me his darkness

i was told he once
spend a year in bed
because a woman
no longer wanted him

(i feel his pain)

he used to write poetry
and my grandad beat the shit
out of him
when he got into
one of his melancholy moods

your father drank
too much whiskey
and he smoked
on construction sites
always hiding
like a pussy

my uncle
tells me things
some times

Rebecca Rijsdijk

and all i think i
how much i am like him
heavy
dark
and victimised

but after i wake up
with a hangover
and after i get dressed
i spend chunks
of my day caring
for the elderly
the marginalised
and the distressed

and when i walk illuminated
my daddy comes back to life
he's a little boy again
and the little boy
still writes his poems
and as i watch him
write his moods away
i want to tell him
he is perfect
when he is sensitive
no matter what anyone says
and please don't ever change

You Were Married When I Met You

To the Bone

how to die a little
on the inside

shut the door
and close your eyes
as you cradle
yourself
on the floor

my love

the concrete is cold
and why are your
eyes leaking

didn't they
tell you
that all you
have to do
is not
let them see
the black
pouring out

to not let them
hear

the sounds
that leave
your mouth
at night
when time
is just this thing
that passes
and wounds
will be wounds
will be wounds

You Were Married When I Met You

Dogs and Masters

i keep
coming back
to you

like a dog
returning
to a master
that kicks it
in the teeth

over
and over
again

i stand there
with my
tail tucked
between
my legs
and my head
hung low

as i desperately
beg for
the scraps
of your love

and i hate
myself for it

You Were Married When I Met You

When Hope is a Lot Like a Loaded Gun

it takes courage to love
she said
and in that moment
what little hope
i had held out for you
died a quiet death
on the bathroom floor

Rebecca Rijsdijk

Truth

at least
your silence
doesn't
lie

You Were Married When I Met You

'Crazy Woman'

never will i
water myself down
for a man again
and if he
that claims
unconditional love
ever is about
to utter
the word
'dramatic'
to describe
my state of being
again
i swear to god
i will rip it out of their
throat before
it ever has the chance
to land anywhere
near my ears
because what
enters the head
will sometimes
live there
forever
and i will just
tell myself

over and over
that i am
in fact
good enough
i am good enough
i am good enough
i
am
more
than
good
enough
i am a raging
burning woman
with a mouth
full of ash
and
you were just
a coward

You Were Married When I Met You

The Fantasy of You and Me

maybe you loved
only the fantasy
of me
suffering artists
are easier
to admire
from a distance
after all
it's all fun
and games
when you don't
have to hold their
mood swings
in your palms
and mop up
their blood
from your
floors

Rebecca Rijsdijk

All was Never Well

i am sorry for
throwing that phone
in your face after i saw
that text to your wife
you know, the one in which
you wrote to her
that you loved her
and missed her
like you had done to me
when it was her bed
you were sleeping in

You Were Married When I Met You

Carpaccio

i went to that place
where you and i
had sandwiches
after you
picked me up
from work one day

you had a meat sandwich
and i had the salmon

the ladies
behind the counter
giggled a lot
when you ordered
our cokes

today i stand
at the counter
alone

what will it be love
the lady asks
without giggling

i look at the salmon
and think of you

carpaccio
i say

You Were Married When I Met You

The Healing

do you smell that
she asks
the earth smells
different
now that the weather
is changing

she passes me
the cigarette we share
with her blond-haired friend
i nod and think
about things
that hardly
seem to matter
like how i never realised
the intimacy
three pairs of lips
on the same
nicotine stained filter
can create

i take another sip
of beer and talk
to the historian
about how
i hadn't

Rebecca Rijsdijk

seen my friend
for years
but how her hair
was still phoenix
red
and
came down
in the same
curly cascades
i had remembered

and for a
second there
i let go
of the fantasy
of you and me
and i am living
in the moment
with my feet
carefully planted
in the early
hours of
the spring
scented soil

You Were Married When I Met You

Not About You

i see my face
reflected
in the back
of a bald men's
head
he's young
there's a scar
in the middle
of his white skin
it reminds me
of the stories
i was told as a child
about the parting
of the red sea
short brown
hair on either
side of it
and i wonder
if someone cried
over him
the way i cry
over you
with a heart
that feels
like screaming
all the damn **time**

Rebecca Rijsdijk

Rejection Abandonment

i think
in the end
it's just me
breaking
my own heart
over and over
again

i am done writing about you now

About the Author

Rebecca Rijsdijk is the author of two other poetry collections; *Portraits of Girls I Never Met* and *The Lady from across the Sea*. She started writing stories as soon as she had learned the alphabet and signed up to study written media at the Academy of Journalism in Tilburg. A brain aneurysm put an end to her journalistic aspirations, however, and words became intertwined with trauma for a while. It wasn't until she completed her degree in design years later, that words started playing a more prominent part in her life again.

Rebecca published *Portraits of Girls* in 2016, not quite knowing what she was actually doing until her friends pointed it out. They understood the poetic nature of her work and recognised reoccurring themes such as love, loss, trauma and dealing with mental health issues.

The Lady from Across the Sea was published in 2018.

Besides writing poems, Rebecca works in healthcare and is currently training to become a nurse.

Recommended Reading

When I first realised I did not love myself like I was supposed too, I was still in the midst of a whirlwind romance with a married man. I googled about being 'the other woman' but only bumped into hateful quotes about homewreckers and whores. I went to therapy, a lot. I worked with several therapists and the last one showed me I am not a witch, I am just having some rejection abandonment wounds. While talking to her, I started reading about trauma. If you are in a similar situation (which I am not saying all 'other women' are), these are the Instagram accounts that helped me, and some books I have on my shelf.

Instagram accounts I follow that deal with empowering women or talk about heartbreak or are just filled with positive vibes that make you feel like you got this:

@risingwoman, @rainbowsalt, @mantramagazine, @the.holistic.psychologist, @m.mustun, @sheleanaaiyana @morganharpernichols, @briannawiest, @lightworkerslounge and *@natlue*

Books that I found helpful relating to the topic:

Mr Unavailable and the Fallback Girl by Natalie Lue
The No Contact Rule by Natalie Lue

Facing Codependence by Pia Mellody
Facing Love Addiction by Pia Mellody
Codependent No More by Melody Beattie
Women Who Love Too Much by Robin Norwood
You're Not Crazy - You're Codependent by Jeanette Elisabeth Menter
All The Reminders You Need To Get You Through Anything In Life by Thought Catalog
The Emotionally Unavailable Man by Patti Henry
This Is Me Letting You Go by Heidi Pricbc
The Strength In Our Scars by Bianca Sparacino
He's Scared, She's Scared by Steven Carter and Julia Sokol
Men Who Can't Love by Steven Carter and Julia Sokol
The Journey from Abandonment to Healing by Susan Anderson
The Body Keeps the Score by Bessel van der Kolk

And in case reading is not enough, here is the web address of the best trauma specialist in London *franproctor.co.uk*. Fran taught me about the toxicity in some of my relationships, and helped me become more emotionally independent. I cannot recommend her enough.

You Were Married
When I Met You

© Rebecca Rijsdijk, 2020

All Rights Reserved.

Written, edited and designed
by Rebecca Rijsdijk

rebeccarysdyk.co.uk
@rebeccarijsdijk

Photo on the Cover
of some innocent bathers
on a vintage photo
I got off of Ebay.

Be kind.